It was sunset
in the jungle,

And the sky was
streaked with red.

The animals
were calling,

It was nearly
time for bed …

It was **bedtime**
in the jungle,

And the **day** was
almost **done**.

A **rhino** lay
down close

to her baby
one.

1

"Sleep," said her mother.

"I'll sleep," said the one.

And they slept in the jungle, as the day was almost done.

It was **bedtime**
in the jungle,

And the **stream** was
shining **blue**.

A **monkey**
made a **bed**

For her babies
two.

2

"Rest," said their mother.

"We'll rest," said the two.

And they rested in their bed, by the stream shining blue.

It was **bedtime**
in the jungle,

And **beneath** a
leafy **tree**

A leopard
tucked her **paws**

Round her babies
three.

"Snuggle," said their mother.

"We'll snuggle," said the three.

And they snuggled up together, beneath the leafy tree.

It was **bedtime**
in the jungle,

And the **sun**
shone no more.

A **wolf**
nuzzled noses

With her babies
four.

4

"Nestle," said their mother.

"We'll nestle," said the four.

And they all began to nestle, as the sun shone no more.

It was **bedtime**
in the jungle,

And the **moon**
would soon arrive.

A **tiger**
gently licked

All her babies
five.

5

"Quiet," said their mother.

"We'll be quiet," said the five.

And they quietly closed their eyes,
as the moon would soon arrive.

It was **bedtime**
in the jungle,

And in a **nest**
of sticks

A **peahen** smoothed
the feathers

of her babies
six.

"Hush," said their mother.

"We'll hush," said the six.

And they hushed side by side, in their nest made of sticks.

It was **bedtime**
in the jungle,

And the **stars shone**
in heaven.

A **wild pig**
snuffled softly

Round her babies
seven.

"Settle," said their mother.

"We'll settle," said the seven.

And they all settled down, as the stars shone in heaven.

It was **bedtime**
in the jungle,

And the **hour** was
getting **late.**

A **duck**
gave a kiss

to her babies
eight.

8

"Cuddle," said their mother.

"We'll cuddle," said the eight.

And they cuddled up close, as the hour was getting late.

It was bedtime
in the jungle,

And the moon
began to shine.

A crocodile
was lazing

With her babies
nine.

9

"Snooze," said their mother.

"We'll snooze," said the nine.

And they all snoozed together, as the moon began to shine.

It was **bedtime**
in the jungle,

And by the
river bend

Elephants were
gathering

all their babies
ten.

10

It was night-time
in the jungle,

And the moon shone
full and bright.

All the
jungle babies

were safely
sleeping tight.